Falsely

Deflow ered

G.S. Riter

Chapter One

Her breath left Penelope in a gasp as her maid, Rose, pulled the strings of her corset tight enough to bruise her ribcage.

"Is this not a mite too tight, Rose?" Penelope questioned through clenched teeth. She had never been a fan of how restrictive women's garments were. One might assume that she was used to it all after twenty years of being stretched, pulled and tightened, but every time, it was a new agony all over again.

"No, My Lady," Rose answered, and Penelope tried to inhale as gingerly as she could. "If I don't bind you tight, your…ah…figure would seem too lush."

And therein lay the whole problem. Penelope had always been 'lush' by society's standards. While she knew that all other women and debutantes had slim, waif-like bodies, hers had always been curvy, and no amount of diet restriction or flat-out starving had been able to change it.

Just the thought of food had her salivating at the mouth. She couldn't even remember the last time she had had a good, warm and crispy slice of bread with butter on top. Her mother was currently on another experiment where she wasn't allowed to have any bread or grain. A few bites of boiled meat and a boiled egg in the morning was all she was supposed to eat.

Just then, on cue, her stomach rumbled loudly. She blushed right down to her toes as Rose let out a chuckle.

"D'you want me to fetch you something from the kitchen?" she asked kindly. "Won't tell no one, My Lady."

Penelope smiled at her maid. She had met Rose in their estate village. She had just been a young widow who needed a shelter and food for her toddler. Something about the woman had drawn Penelope in and she had told her mother that she wanted Rose as her maid. It hadn't been an easy recruitment as her mother had objected vehemently, but she had to give in eventually because once Penelope decided something, she did it no matter what.

The first year had been a learning experience for both Penelope and Rose as they had discovered so many new things together. Suffice it to say, now Penelope and Rose were both well-accomplished in all things required of a lady's maid. Trying to make sure that her mother found no reason to sever Rose's employment, who had become a close friend and confidant, Penelope had learned quite a few things herself too.

"I'm fine," Penelope sighed, returning to the moment and staring in the mirror at her reflection. Her auburn curls, another thing that separated her from the ton and the current fashion, were swept back and cascaded down her back in loose curls. Rose had made sure to brush them until they shone and her efforts had paid off. They reached almost to her hip and while they were another thing her mother really worried about, Penelope found them the best aspect of her appearance.

Her large jade-colored eyes were bracketed by red lashes and her petite nose was adorned with a cluster of freckles— ones that did not go away no matter how many bonnets she wore or lemons she applied to her skin. Her heart-shaped face, arched eyebrows, and perfectly bow-shaped lips may have passed her off as a beauty if it hadn't been for her curvy figure. Penelope knew that she wasn't fat by any means, but her body type was a rare one, one that 'milkmaids' had, as her mother called it.

"I don't want you to faint there at the ball," Rose frowned. She had never agreed with any of Penelope's mother's vehement attempts to slim her down and had told Penelope that more times than she could count.

"I won't faint," Penelope assured her. "Not due to hunger at least," she murmured to herself.

"What do you mean?" Rose frowned, and Penelope shook her head.

"Why won't my brother listen to me?" Rose sighed in dejection. The corset tightened immediately and she had to straighten up. "This will kill me for sure," she grumbled, reminding herself to take smaller breaths.

"Now you are being ungrateful. He wants you to enjoy your own season, experience everything, and choose a husband who deserves you. Is that really a crime?" Rose grumbled as she fretted about a stray lock of her hair that had escaped the arrangement.

"Not really, but should I not have a say in all this? What if I don't want to have a season? I know everything there is to it and I am fine without living it firsthand," Penelope tried to explain, the topic mounting her anxiety once again.

"Knowing it and living it are two different things and what is really going on? I had discounted all your previous complaints but now I'm thinking something other than your books is keeping you from wanting to have your own season," Rose worried as she looked into Penelope's eyes in the mirror.

To her mother's disgust and her brother's worry, Penelope was an avid reader. When she had tired of being chastised for her appetite as a youngster, she had taken solace in the library. Soon enough, books had become her saviors and the characters had become her only friends. And while the habit had been appreciated by her tutors and her governess when she had been a girl, it had very easily turned into a bad habit in her mother's opinion.

"I'm alright Rose. Please don't worry. Let's just get this ball over with." Penelope straightened her shoulders and tried to bring forth all the strength she could muster.

Rose did not look convinced if the expression on her face was anything to go by, but it was because she knew Penelope well. Anyone who didn't would only see a proud, confident, and breathtakingly beautiful young woman descending the

stairs when her name was called out loudly
in the crowded ballroom.

Chapter Two

The Marsden ball was in full swing and Stephen Debrett, Marquess of Winchester couldn't have been more bored if he had tried. It was his first ball of the season and he was only in attendance because the invitation had been a personal one. John Marsden was one of his closest and possibly only friend in the world and there was no way Stephen could have ignored the summons from such a close friend. He had arrived late, or as fashionably late as he could have, but even that didn't seem to help him.

"Lord Winchester," someone called out loudly, making Stephen turn from his spot right along the very fringes of the ballroom. He had already garnered a lot of attention when his name had been announced and since he didn't want to steal the spotlight from John's sister, he had decided to spend the rest of the evening in seclusion.

"Williams," Stephen looked at the man who had made him turn and nodded stiffly. 'Williams' was actually Scott Douglas, a Baron and the most pompous person in London Society. Stephen's disregard and failure to offer Lord Williams the full courtesy of his title had the other man visibly straightening up and the otherwise pleasant expression on his face turning to an embarrassed shade of red.

"To whom do we owe the pleasure of your company today?" Williams asked, almost through gnashed teeth as he struggled to maintain the smile on his face. "A debutante ball is the last thing anyone could've expected you to attend."

The last sentence was said with as much mockery as possible and Stephen knew well what Williams implied, but he was too old and too smart to take petty baits men dished out to him regularly. He had long ago gotten over the ridicule and mockery, and every person who had once made fun of him and his past had had to eat their words sooner or later when they had needed his influence and his expertise, so he let small words slide by easily.

"I didn't realize you or anyone had certain expectations when it came to me," he replied with a raised brow and continued to sip from the tumbler of scotch he had in his hand, surveying the dance floor and dismissing Williams in a single minute.

"Well, as far as debutante balls are concerned, you have probably chosen the best one yet," Williams spoke, unaffected. "I've heard that the Lady Marsden is quite a delicious morsel." He grinned, and Stephen's lips tightened in distaste.

If anyone heard the discussions that went on in the supposedly 'sophisticated' society, they would be shocked. He had spent time on both sides of the society and had met some of the best people in the otherwise 'unsophisticated' lot and the worst scoundrels in the decent one. It was easy to evaluate that money, power and entitlement did little to change the basic nature of a man.

"I've not had the good fortune to meet the *lady*," he replied tersely, stressing on the last word so Williams would know that he was not up for any vile discussions and comments on the person of Lady Penelope Marsden. John had told him quite a bit about his sister and Stephen had seen her around when she had been a young girl. He hadn't met her in a long time so he didn't know how the little bookworm they had always encountered in the library looked now, but what little he did know about her was enough to tell him that she was a sensible young woman and not one of the simpering and shy misses one usually encountered at the marriage mart.

"I think I'll go check her out right now, she seems to be standing all alone, bored at her own ball," Williams chuckled. Something about his words or his manner rubbed Stephen the wrong way and before he knew what was happening, the words were spilling from his mouth.

"She owes me her next dance," he announced, and without waiting for a reply, strode in the direction of John's younger sister.

He had taken almost ten steps when he realized he didn't know what she looked like. Roving his eyes over the ballroom, he then tried to match all the ladies present to the image of the girl he had seen at the Marsden Manor. While no one really matched any of his estimations, he couldn't help but appreciate a lone woman standing at the far corner of the ballroom. She looked like she was hiding from everyone. Giving up his search for just a moment, he concentrated on the woman. She interested him somewhat and that was the exact moment that the woman moved, her body coming out from the behind the curtain she had been hiding behind, and Stephen gulped.

Good God, he thought. The rich, voluptuous body of the woman in question was enough to have men salivating after her. Unlike all the other ladies, she had lush curves, the cut of the gown only emphasizing her spectacular figure—and combined with the refreshing innocence he saw on her face, he was awestruck for just a moment.

"Winchester," someone suddenly pounded him on the back. "You came."

Stephen turned around reluctantly and gave John an answering pat on the back. His tongue burned to ask his oldest friend about the woman he had just seen but he decided to hold back his tongue right then.

"How could I not?" He smiled at John. He was the only person he ever smiled at. Even his servants noticed that. His valet, who had been an old acquaintance, had suggested more than enough times for him to smile a little more and dislodge the title of 'The Cold Marquess' but Stephen actually enjoyed the mystery and the little fear people felt from him.

"I'm so glad and thankful. Right now, I have another favor to ask," John sighed, and Stephen finally noticed the worry lines on his friend's face.

"What is it?" he asked immediately.

"Penelope told me time and again
that she didn't want the hassle of a season
and I didn't listen. I have now watched her
alone and more despondent than ever since
the ball has started," John explained. "It is
making me think that maybe she had been
right."

"Why is she alone?" Stephen asked,
unable to understand. The ball had been for
Penelope so he couldn't understand why
she was lonely while everyone else enjoyed
it.

"The damned society and its
preferences," John muttered. "Most of the
men look for shy, waif-like, young wives.
Penelope is already twenty-two since she
had to remain in mourning—first for my
father and then my idiot brother's death.
Now she is not only aged, but she also isn't
exactly thin and waif-like. And her dowry is
not as extensive as many of the other

debutantes this season," he finished with a weary tone.

"Good grief," Stephen rolled his eyes. "How come a man is just a young buck when he is twenty-two and a woman is considered old at the same age?"

"We just have too many prejudices," John replied, and Stephen shook his head.

And people ask me what I have against the ton, he thought with disgust, feeling bad for John who not only was leaden with the duty of his sister but also the dwindling affairs of his estate that his father and brother had almost left in ruins.

"Right now, I just want you to ask her for a dance," John finally told him. "And try to lighten her up while you are at it. I'm hoping you dancing with her might just improve her position in the eyes of the bachelors."

"Sure, I was already looking for her," Stephen remembered, and told his friend. "Just point her out to me and I'll go and ask the girl to dance."

"Thank you," John smiled, and his tight shoulders dropped a little. "There she is holding on to that curtain for dear life," he said, moving his head slightly to the right and motioning towards the other end of the ballroom.

Stephen had all but forgotten about the gorgeous woman he had been eyeing before John had interrupted him until his friend pointed towards the very same woman. His own mouth fell open in shock.

"That is your little sister?" he asked John with equal parts incredulity and shock.

The lady in question was no little girl, she was all woman and Stephen's mood instantly plummeted as he realized that the first woman to have stolen his attention in a

long time was not just gorgeous but also
way out of his reach.

Chapter Three

Penelope felt tears gather at the corners of her eyes as the harsh words spoken by women she had never met fell on her ears. She was standing at the threshold of the powder room from where unfiltered laughter poured out at regular intervals.

After the lecherous expressions but otherwise very clear rebukes she had suffered from the men, she had decided to pluck up some courage and try her hand at making some friends out of the women but it had been such a long time that she had forgotten that women were just as cruel if not more so than the men. Monikers and names were rampant on the tongues of everyone as her worst nightmares were all realized in the span of one small ball.

Dejected and ordering herself not to cry, Penelope whirled around and decided to go back to the safety of her room, the ball be damned. So immersed in her thoughts was she that she didn't see the man standing in her path and collided with him.

Two large, strong hands came to rest on her arms just above her elbows, and the warmth emanating from the large male body and the hands caused a shiver to run through Penelope's spine. Ignoring her body's reaction and embarrassed at the shriek that she had almost emitted, she raised her head to look at the face that belonged to the massive body.

While she hadn't had enough exposure to the male species to judge what women meant when they called certain men handsome, Penelope was sure that the face she was looking at was one of the most striking ones she had ever seen in her life.

Chiseled bone structure, strong thick brows, long lashes, and inky black hair. Along with the tanned complexion and a body that screamed of leashed power, it was an intense combination.

Completing her perusal of the man's features and giving due attention to his wide and full lips, Penelope finally looked into his eyes. They were such a shock that she almost gasped. Molten silver.

Ringed with black and specks of a very light ice-blue, the color was unlike any she had ever seen. The gaze and the heavy lids made him seem like a predator and Penelope found it hard to control her heartbeat.

"If you have looked your fill and are sure that you won't fall, I would like to let you go." As the man spoke, his rough, deep voice flowed through her body, lighting up several nerve endings on its way.

"I—I'm sorry," she stuttered, her brain finally catching up with what he had said, and she quickly took a step back.

"No need to apologize. I'm Stephen Debrett, a friend of your brother's," he announced, and Penelope suddenly had a flashback of a very serious and short-tempered young man who had come home often with her brother John from Eton. She was also surprised that Stephen had announced himself as her brother's friend rather than his title, like most gentlemen.

Remembering her manners, Penelope went down in a deep curtsy and offered him a slight smile. "My Lord."

She didn't say anything else because she was sure that John would've mentioned the woes of having a difficult sister and all her issues to his closest friend and she didn't want to face any of those things right then. She opened her mouth to excuse herself when he spoke up.

"May I have this dance?"

Her eyes all but popped out of their sockets as she comically looked at his offered hand and then at his face. She might not have acted that way normally but all the rejections since the start of the ball had not put her in the best of moods and she was shocked that this handsome man wanted to dance with her.

Narrowing her eyes, she started to look at her surroundings.

"My brother put you up to this, didn't he?" she asked with a defeated sigh, the tears once again threatening her eyes. She wasn't sure if she was more angry at her brother, or ashamed that he now had to beg his friends to ask his pathetic little sister to dance.

The next thing she knew her wrist was ensnared in one of the large hands that had been on her arm a moment ago, and she was being pulled in the direction of the dance floor.

"No one can make me do something I don't want to do," was whispered in the same gravelly and serious voice right next to her ear as she was expertly pulled into a waltz.

The next few minutes were some of the best moments of Penelope's life. She loved to dance and when one's partner was as much of an expert as Lord Winchester, there was no way to not enjoy it. He was silent throughout the dance but his moves and his skills more than made up for it and Penelope had no cause to complain when the dance was over, though it was much sooner than she would have liked.

Her partner bowed and directly moved towards the door, leaving her breathless and the center of attention.

~~~

"I heard you had a good time at the ball last night," Rose said the next morning as she brought her breakfast in bed.

Penelope rubbed the sleep from her eyes and gave her an amused glance.

"Oh really? And where did you hear that from?" she asked with a smile. "Mother?"

Rose colored slightly, and Penelope knew that she had hit the mark.

"I had such an awful time Rose. I don't want to attend another ball, ever," she groaned as she took a sip of her tea.
~~~

"But I was told you danced and had a great time," Rose frowned, worry evident in her voice.

"I had three dances and the last two were just because of Lord Winchester's waltz. The very one John forced him to dance with me." She rolled her eyes, the tea tasting bitter on her tongue.

"Now, now. The good Lord might have asked you out of his own choice," Rose chastised, and Penelope shook her head.

"Let's not lie to each other Rose. We both know that the ball was an utter flop even after Mother's continuous tries and John almost begging his friends to dance with me," she said in a fake chipper voice. Penelope didn't want Rose or anyone else to see how much the ball and the people had affected her.

"It will get better," Rose tried to reassure her, but Penelope wasn't hopeful in the least. She just wanted to be done with the season without any other such events that drew attention towards her.

Chapter Four

"This ball is such a hit, all it needs is a juicy scandal," said Viscount Pemberley. Stephen simply rolled his eyes. The middle-aged, balding Viscount was as ridiculous as his name. If it weren't for the lack of company, Stephen would never have let the man stay close to him for too long.

To his growing weariness, he had realized that the Viscount not only loved to gossip like a woman, he also expected the other person to participate.

"Well, sure," Stephen answered his expectant smile and Pemberley frowned, probably finding his answer and enthusiasm about the matter inadequate but that was the best Stephen could do under the circumstances. He was bored and irritable as hell.

Another ball was the last thing he had wanted to come to, especially after what had happened at the last one. His valet had gleefully told him how the scandal sheets had gone wild with stories of 'The Cold Marquess and The Inappropriate Debutante'. He had no objections to what they had written about him but reading all the rubbish written about Penelope Marsden had made him surprisingly angry. He had assured himself that it was because she was the sister of his closest friend and he felt protective about her after all John had just informed him this very morning that he was seriously looking to accept the very next proposal for his sister's hand.

The man had been very worried and Stephen, with his limited knowledge of the ton, had been unable to understand why Penelope hadn't already been snatched up by some fortunate bloke. If he was asked, she was the best pick of this season or more like every season he had attended events of. Her uniqueness and freshness were such a pull that ever since the ball had started, he had been unable to control his own eyes from seeking her out from amongst the crush.

He was yet to lay his eyes on her and that was another reason he was irritated but he was never going to admit that, not to anyone or even himself.

"….the young Lady Marsden."

Stephen had been so lost in thoughts that he had tuned out the Viscount but his ears suddenly decided to take interest as the man took Penelope's name.

"What did you say?" He asked sharply. Pemberley just stared at him as if he had grown horns.

"Just that our good old Williams seems to be really after this Lady Marsden

I've heard," Pemberley repeated and Stephen couldn't stop the frown that appeared on his forehead.

"Williams Douglas?" He asked, just to be sure. Williams was just a Baron and in his opinion, not at all worthy of Penelope.

"Yes," Pemberley grew excited, realizing that he had finally discovered the topic Stephen had some interest in. "Just yesterday, someone saw them disappearing together towards one of the alcoves."

Stephen suddenly had the urge to go look for this Williams and drive his hand through the man's jaw.

"Who?" He asked tersely, trying to keep his voice under control and not give the chronic gossiper any ammunition.

"Who?" Pemberley repeated, confused.

"Who saw them?" He asked. He wanted to be sure that the information was correct. He wasn't sure why verifying the information was important to him but right then, it just was.

Pemberley had just opened his mouth to answer him when there were a sudden shout and the next thing he knew, people were moving towards the East terrace quickly, the whispers and excited voices rising quite a few octaves.

"Oh, a scandal!" Pemberley almost shouted in joy and dove towards the terrace, pushing people out of the way actively.

Stephen wasn't interested in what had happened, only irritated that his question wasn't answered and had just decided to go home when some of the whispers reached his ears.

"She probably did it on purpose, knowing that there was no other to secure a match what with that vulgar figure of hers," a pair of women close to him were murmuring conspiratorily. There was such scorn in their voices but that wasn't what had Stephen's heart beating out of control. He had started to suddenly have a really bad feeling about it all and before he knew, he was shoving people out of his way and moving towards the damned terrace.

He wasn't a very religious man but when he was just a few people away from the scene of the scandal, he sent up a silent prayer both for his friend and for himself, hoping against everything that he was wrong.

Williams Douglas was the first person he saw as the people moved to let him move forward. He was standing in front of a woman and looking all but proud and joyful as he announced,

"She just said yes to my proposal of marriage. We were celebrating when you gentlemen interrupted. I'm sure you can understand that we are young and things sometimes tend to get out of hand," He grinned as he said that.

Unable to wait anymore, Stephen moved forward until he was able to clearly see a shock of auburn hair glinting red in the light of the terrace. As his eyes fell on the huddled figure behind Williams Douglas, he suddenly felt rage so extreme, it was the greatest test in patience that he was able to control it.

"What is going on here?" He asked, his voice coming out clipped and as cold as the moniker they had given him. Everyone suddenly quietened and for the first time since he had come upon the scene, he saw Williams look a little uneasy.

"Nothing my Lord. I and my fiancée were just..," He started to say but Stephen held up a hand.

"Is that Lady Penelope Marsden?" he asked, even though he knew that she was. There was no one else with that hair or that body, the very same one he had been unable to forget for most of the week.

"Yes," Williams announced, his shoulders broadening as he said that.

"Her brother is my closest friend and he didn't mention any betrothal when I met him this morning," He said, looking Williams in the eyes. The younger man almost squirmed as he answered.

"I just asked," he started to say, and Stephen stopped him once again.

"There is no betrothal until the papers are signed and the matter has been discussed with her brother. Right now, I will just take her home. You are welcome to visit her brother with the offer in the morning," The last sentence came out as almost a growl as Stephen quickly moved forward. And before anyone could protest, he hauled Penelope out from behind Williams and started walking towards the door of the ballroom, not looking back at all of the shocked faces that he left behind.

Chapter Five

Penelope was so cold. It seemed as if the cold had seeped directly into her bones and nothing was ever going to chase it away. She was sitting in the Marquess Debrett's carriage as the owner sat next to her, as still as a stone. The man didn't even move when the carriage passed over the rough patches in the road, as still as a marble statue.

Penelope was afraid to look at him, barely holding on to her tears and emotions on a tight leash. She didn't want to break down in front of him and embarrass herself if such a thing was even possible anymore. It was the worst day of her life, she thought as she closed her eyes tightly to hold back the tears.

If she had expected to ask any questions, comfort her or even ask if what Williams had said was true, she would've been sorely disappointed. He was probably just taking her home because of his kinship to her brother but nevertheless, she was grateful. If he hadn't arrived right then at the terrace, she didn't know what she would've done.

It all seemed like a nightmare, one she would give anything to forget about. The carriage suddenly stopped and the movement had her jerking out of the seat towards the opposite side. She would've fallen onto the carriage floor if it wasn't for the two strong and now familiar hands, holding onto her shoulder.

She was just about to turn and thank him when he adjusted her brusquely and moved away.

"We've arrived."

The words were clipped and closed all doors for any sort of conversation Penelope had had in her mind. For the first time since he had dragged her off the ball, she realized that his expression was cancerous and savage, no familiarity to the serious but peaceful man she had danced with just a week ago. The tears threatened again and she quickly got out of the carriage, not waiting for the driver to help her out.

The door of her brother's townhouse was already open and Charles, their butler stood there, a confused expression on his face.

"Tell your master I wish to see him immediately!" the Marquess barked orders as he waited for her to enter first. Instead of waiting for her brother, Penelope all but ran up the stairs towards her room. She wasn't sure how long she could keep her torn gown together and hide its condition from The Marquess and her brother both.

It had been dark in the carriage and the Marquess probably hadn't been able to see how the torn gown had gaped at the bodice when she had almost fallen to the floor. While she was determined to tell John the truth about what had happened, she didn't want to explain it in front of the frigid Marquess and his judgmental gaze.

I'll change and then go down to tell John everything, Penelope thought as she opened the door of her room and quickly set to changing her clothes without the help of Rose. Once she was done, she rushed to her brother's study only for the butler to tell her that John had asked to not be disturbed at all costs.

The Marquess was still inside and Penelope decided to wait. Five minutes turned into fifteen, a half hour and finally a full one hour. Restlessness and fear about what John would think had her immobilized as the Charles and Rose both came to her at intervals, asking her to go to her room and talk to her brother in the morning.

William's words about their betrothal kept ringing in her ears and she was scared that John was going to believe those very words and actually agree to the marriage. There had been no other offers and after today, she was sure that there were never going to be any.

Don't you dare cry Penelope, she reminded herself as Rose looked at her in sympathy and resignation.

"He'll call you when he's done I'm sure," she tried to get her to move again. "Your lips are almost blue with the cold and it's very late. Go and rest for a bit, please."

"You will call me when he's done?" Penelope asked, realizing that she was worried about both Charles and Rose with her behavior.

"Yes, I promise," Rose sighed.

"Where's Mother?" Penelope asked, gulping as her voice came out in a whisper.

"She's sleeping in her room. I'll tell the staff not to mention anything to her until you or your brother have had a chance to talk," Rose assured her. "Go to your room now."

Penelope nodded and went up the stairs, reassuring herself that there was no way that tomorrow could be worse than the day she had already passed. The next day she realized that one should never tempt fate.

Chapter Six

Stephen had a blazing headache when he woke up next morning and all the events of the previous day rushed back to him. He had returned from John's townhouse three hours past midnight and had then proceeded to drink his weight in scotch.

"This is for your headache My Lord," Bennet, his butler, announced motioning towards a disgusting-looking drink in a tall glass. The sight of the brew made Stephen groan when he was sure that it would have any other man running for the hills, swearing to never touch a bottle of scotch again.

"You sure know how to torture a man, Bennet," he said, disgusted after downing the contents of the glass in one big gulp.

"I noticed that you succeeded in cleaning up half of your collection of scotch. May I enquire what the matter was?" Bennet asked. Stephen knew that the question was one no valet would have the audacity to ask his master, but Bennet was first a friend and then his valet and right then, it was his friend who was asking him the question.

"Well, since you asked so nicely," Stephen smiled a huge fake smile before he dropped a literal bomb. "It seems like I'll be getting married by the end of this week."

The glass Bennet had been holding in his hand fell down and shattered to a tiny million fragments but the man never even blinked, looking at him in such shock that it would've been comical if Stephen wasn't feeling the bitter effect of the words after they left his tongue.

"You're getting married?" Bennet asked, his voice coming out in a squeak and Stephen rolled his eyes.

"Yes, that's what I said," he answered irritably, wrapping his body in his wrapper and moving towards the warm bath he knew Bennet would have readied for him before he woke up.

"You're getting married?" Bennet asked again, standing in the same position with the broken glass at his feet and his hand still in midair.

"Okay now this is getting ridiculous," Stephen growled, disgusted. "What is so shocking about me getting married? I'm sure that you knew it was going to happen one day," he snapped, irritated.

"I knew no such thing," Bennet finally unfroze and turned around, a scowl on his face.

"What do you mean? You thought I was never going to marry?" Stephen asked, disbelief coloring his tone. "That's absurd."

"No, it is not absurd. All of us down below had placed bets a long time ago and I had won," His valet said as if it made perfect sense and he was actually offended that Stephen was getting married.

"What were the odds?" Stephen asked eyes narrowed as he contemplated that his own servants had placed bets on if he was going to die a bachelor.

"There were no odds. All of us won," Bennet smirked, and Stephen's brows went up.

"You mean all of your bet that I was going to die alone?" he scowled. "I'm offended that none of you know how to place a bet. You see, there are supposed to be two different," he started to explain when he noticed the small smile on Bennet's face and broke off.

"We know how to place bets." His valet rolled his eyes. "It was just that no one thought you will ever marry," he completed. Stephen was just about to say something else in his defense when Bennet spoke again, all traces of humor gone from his eyes, replaced by hope and happiness.

"Who is the unfortunate lady?" he asked, but the words contradicted the happiness Stephen saw inside his eyes.

"Unfortunate indeed," he murmured, guilt swamping him again.

The feeling that he should never have listened to John started to creep into his mind again and he shut his eyes to ward it off.

It has already happened, nothing to be done about it now, he reminded himself.

"What happened?" Bennet asked, the happiness having faded to wariness and Stephen couldn't control it anymore. The words spilled from his lips of their own accord as he told him about what had happened at the ball and then how John had all but begged him to sign his betrothal papers to Penelope. He hadn't wanted to, the anger of the evening still fresh in his mind but then John had reminded him about his debt to him. John had been his only friend and savior from the bullies and the rascals back at Eton. He had been a late bloomer, looking ten when he had been thirteen years of age. That and his past had made him an easy target for all the bullies. John had stepped in one day and they had been inseparable ever since. Stephen had never said anything, but he did feel as if John had played a major part in shaping him into who he was today. How could he have refused such a friend the only thing he had ever asked?

"But, what about the lady?" Bennet asked shocked. "If she really does love that other fellow?"

"No sane woman can fall in love with Williams Douglas," Stephen spat, angry. "And she barely knows him for a week. It is at most a silly infatuation. John says that the lady has been sheltered all her life and he doesn't want her to make such a huge mistake."

"I understand that but if she really does love him?" Bennet asked again.

"Well then, I am pretty much doomed my friend," Stephen chuckled bitterly.

He had never really thought about marriage, the prospect always seems like it was too far into the future to even consider right then but when he did think about it, he had never thought about a wife whose heart belonged to another man.

"I just need an heir and then she'll be free to do whatever she pleases," he said sharply. He had come to that conclusion during the heavy drinking the night before. He did think that John was making a mistake by not consulting Penelope before signing her betrothal papers, but he didn't fault the man. If it had been his sister, he would have been doing everything to drive her away from a lecherous fellow like Williams.

The man was not just obnoxious and cunning, he had no respect whatsoever for women. Stephen himself had heard and seen him treat women in the worst way possible and if that wasn't enough, he was also known to be a heavy gambler and was elbows deep in debt and probably headed to the debtor's prison soon. That was probably why he had targeted Penelope. While her dowry wasn't excessive, it was still ample and combined with her beauty, Stephen knew that it was a temptation no man would ignore.

While men rebuked and rejected Penelope at the balls, Stephen knew that every man with two functioning eyes thought that she was gorgeous in every way a woman needed to be.

"I really don't think this is a good idea," Bennet brought him out of his thoughts with his words. His forehead was creased with worry and his mouth was tight.

"Good idea or not, it is done. The lady would be marrying me by the end of this week and I'll be damned if I let her go after signing those betrothal papers," Stephen answered determined.

It was probably his ego that kept him from telling his friend and his valet about the huge burden that he felt had been lifted from his chest ever since he had signed the papers. He had first felt the load when she had seen that shiny red hair behind Williams and the load had made breathing slightly difficult. Just slightly.

Chapter Seven

"You look gorgeous," Rose said, her voice trembling as tears covered her eyes and threatened to fall down. Penelope knew that she should be feeling emotional and teary-eyed too, but she couldn't muster up any emotion right then.

"I always knew you'll be a beautiful bride," Rose said, fussing with her hair for the millionth time as she prepared to place the hip-length veil over her head. The dress was the simplest Penelope could find and she was bound tighter in her corset that she had ever been, making sure that she wouldn't be able to sit down at all.

Should've known that leaving the dress in mother's hand would be the worst thing I could've done for myself, she thought dispassionately. The satin dress was such a tight fit that there was no way she could've worn that without cinching the corset as tight as possible.

"Did you talk to John?" she asked Rose, and her maid sighed. It wasn't the first time she had asked her that. When she had first realized that her brother wasn't going to talk to her, she had grown frantic but none of her struggles and tantrums had penetrated the sturdy walls of his studies where he seemed to be camped since the past whole week. She wasn't allowed inside and the only time she had seen him come out of there was when he had told her that he expected her to make no further spectacle of herself and marry Stephen Debrett, The Cold Marquess, in a private and small ceremony by the end of the week.

Right then, she had been too shocked to say anything but by the time she had recovered, John had already gone back inside and had strictly ordered no one to disturb him. That was the last time she had seen him though she had heard that Williams had arrived right on time the morning after the dratted ball and had all been thrown out on his ear after being informed of her betrothal to Stephen Debrett. That news had been the only highlight of her week.

"Your brother doesn't seem to want to talk to anyone, not even your mother," Rose said with a raised brow.

"He believed what Williams said, didn't he?" she finally asked Rose. The question had been bothering her since he had announced her betrothal but she had avoided thinking about it, not wanting to shatter any illusions that her brother trusted her, but it seemed quite possible to her then.

"I don't think so," Rose answered too quickly and Penelope knew that she was lying.

"Do you believe me?" she asked, feeling betrayed and broken inside. She couldn't remember the last time she had felt worse, not even when her father had died of a heart attack or when her eldest brother had been shot in an illegal duel over a game of cards, a shoulder wound ending up in his death.

"Of course, I do Pen," Rose answered honestly, calling her 'Pen' just as she used to when they had first met and her mother hadn't forced Rose to start calling her 'My Lady'.

"Why doesn't John then?" she asked, her voice breaking at the last word and Rose quickly moved forward, raising her face and making her look her in the eyes.

"This is not the time for self-pity Penelope. I have always liked your fighting spirit and your resilience. Don't break down now. This wedding is taking place no matter what and the sooner you put the past behind you, the easier your life will be," Rose whispered, her hand still on Penelope's cheeks.

"But, he probably hates me Rose," Penelope gulped, her own voice coming out a whisper.

"You don't know that and even if it's true, he doesn't know the truth. Your brother thinks that he's an honorable man and I believe him," Rose said, her voice getting firmer. "He will find out the truth and everything will be okay. Marriages have a way of working out," she smiled.

Penelope inhaled deeply and tried not to think about anything after that. The next hour passed in a blur and soon it was time for the ceremony. John finally materialized then, told her she looked beautiful and proceeded to lead her to the altar. Penelope felt as if she was having an out of body experience as if everything was happening to someone else and she was just a spectator.

She only came to life when the priest asked her if she took Stephen Debrett as her lawfully wedded husband. Her pause must've been too long because her bridegroom squeezed her hands tightly and she gasped, looked into his eyes for the first time since the ceremony had started and found anger apparent in them. Her 'I do' was more of a stutter than a declaration as she gazed into the molten silver eyes of her husband, hypnotized and unable to look away.

"You may kiss the bride," the priest announced finally and Penelope prepared to turn her face away slightly so he could kiss her on the cheek instead of the lips when her new husband shocked her by cupping her face in both his hands and keeping it in place as he swooped down and took her lips with his own.

Penelope stood immobilized, frozen in shock as his hands moved from her shoulder to her waist and he drew her in more tightly to his body. Her hands came up to his chest to push him off but tightened on his lapels instead as he changed the angle of the kiss and suddenly swiped his tongue across her closed lips. Penelope gasped, her face turning red at the thought of their audience but the next moment, her mind was cleared of all thoughts as his tongue entered her open mouth, caressing and entwining with her tongue.

The action caused a bright flash of heat to pass through her body and she softened, curiosity getting the better of her and her own tongue moving to touch his.

His groan finally penetrated the fog of passion that had clouded her brain and her pushed back with all her might, only managing to move him back a few inches. Both of them were breathing heavily, her husband's eyes a hot silver as he looked at her lips and then back at her eyes.

"I had hoped this might help to remind you about who you have actually married," he murmured too low for anyone to hear, but Penelope heard the undercurrent of anger in his tone.

"I didn't–" she started to say but he silenced her by tightening his arms around her waist and closing the distance of the few inches between them again.

"No lies, wife," he said, the last word delivered in a mocking tone. For the first time in days, Penelope felt anger replacing the desolation in her heart and mind and she stood up straighter and took a firm step back.

"Duly noted, husband," she replied in the same scathing tone and then walked down the altar and out of the church alone, not even noticing the shocked expressions on her family's faces or the grin on her husband's.

Chapter Eight

Stephen couldn't wait for the wedding breakfast to be done and over with. His stiff cravat had started to seem like a noose and the dining table a prison. The feeling of claustrophobia and not being able to control the situation was a new one for him. He had last felt that way when he had been a boy of mere seven years old and his master, the person who had been everything to him for as far as he could remember, had told him that his 'real father' had 'bought' him. That day when he had boarded the carriage and the motion had made him feel sick because it had been his first time, he had sworn to himself that he would never feel that way again.

But, here he was now, surrounded by idle chatter, merry laughter and curious gazes not knowing how to control what had happened or how to even meet the eyes of the woman he had married, the one who loved someone else.

I should never have let John talk me into this, he thought to himself as the first drop of sweat descended from his temple.

Penelope, his wife, didn't notice anything. It was probably because she had not even looked at him once ever since they had left the church. There were a few times that her family had tried to engage her in their conversations, but she hadn't even looked up, her plate sat empty and if Stephen hadn't heard the occasional indrawn breath, he would've been sure that she had turned to stone.

He sneaked a look towards her once again, disgusted by his own lack of control once again. Penelope looked like an angel, one descended directly from heaven with the sole purpose of torturing him and he had to hand it to her, she had done a brilliant job of it. He snorted at the thought.

That is exactly when his new wife turned to look at him for the first time since they had said their vows. Her bright green eyes with a golden ring around the iris had him mesmerized for a moment and that was probably why he only noticed the sheen of tears in her eyes after she had turned back her head.

The lady is crying on the occasion of her wedding breakfast, he thought with a self-deprecating smirk. It was another few hours before the guests started filtering out. By the time that happened, Stephen had resorted to sharp nods and glares and the wine had been replaced by old scotch in his hand. His anger with himself and his situation had combined with reluctant attraction and lust for his wife as he saw her talking with others, smiling occasionally and just standing in one place looking like his very own brand of hell.

When the last guest left, Stephen was fuming mad, partially aroused already and well on his way to getting drunk. Penelope had been shown to her room almost an hour ago and he had given strict instructions to the servants and his housekeeper to make sure that she was comfortable because no matter what, she was his wife now and he did not want the world to know that everything wasn't completely fine between them.

"Victor!" he called out to the stable hand who was busy helping the rest of the servants carry some of the gifts and rearrange the furniture.

"Yes, My Lord?" the young boy hurried towards him.

"Leave all this. The others will manage, your duty is in the stable," he said crisply and the boy almost turned red, "Go and ready my horse, I'll be taking a short trip around town."

"Today?" Victor asked, eyes wide and mouth hanging open.

"What is wrong with today?" Stephen asked irritably.

"N-nothing at all, I'll get the horse," the boy stammered and dashed off. Stephen sighed and was just about to follow the boy out of the house when the thoughts that had been plaguing him since the morning gained more fervor. Abruptly, he turned around and climbed the stairs two at the time, stopping only when he reached the Marchioness's bedroom adjacent to his very own.

Not bothering to knock, he opened the door and strode inside. Penelope was sitting in front of the dresser and her maid, who looked like she had been brushing her hair, was now just standing there looing at him with wide eyes.

What is with all this surprise? he thought, annoyed. *This is my wife's bedroom, they should've been expecting me to come.*

"Leave us," he said to the gawking maid before turning back to his wife and just looking at her, waiting for the maid to shut the door behind her.

"Husband," Penelope murmured, standing up and rounding the chair until she came into view completely.

Stephen's tongue suddenly dried up and he was pretty sure a few of his neurons fired off spontaneously as he found himself taking a few steps until he stood in front of Penelope.

"Wife," he murmured then. If he had thought that she had looked like an angel at the wedding, he wasn't sure what to compare her to right then. She had her luscious body encased in a flowing and form-hugging silver gown. The gown was cinched at the waist and drew his gaze to her small waist, flaring hips and ample bosom. The silver also brought out the red of her hair and the green of her eyes making her appear like a wild creature, something right out of fairytales.

Unbidden, his hand rose to sweep a strand that had fallen in front of her eye as she had looked at him when he had called her 'wife'. His fingers glided over the smooth skin, moving from her temples and following the path of the strand, going over her cheek and then moving lower until they were at her soft and plump lips.

Penelope took in a sharp breath when his finger caressed her lower lip, moved to her chin and then finally the slope of her swan-line neck until they rested of the neckline of her gown. In all his exploration, he had moved even closer to her and now the heat of her body radiated towards him and they were touching almost hip to hip.

"You-," Penelope started to say something after gulping a few times and her incomplete word finally pulled him out of the stupor he had gone in. He cleared his own throat and took a step back, his body and his fingers both feeling the loss of contact immediately, longing becoming a sudden part of his blood.

"I just wanted to see if you've settled in well," he said, looking anywhere but at Penelope as he said that and then pivoted on his heels to stride out of the room the same way he had come in.

"W-won't you stay?" The almost whispered words stopped him in his track and while his body and his mind rebelled,

he turned around, looked his wife in the
eyes and said,

"No."

Chapter Nine

Penelope stood in her place, almost as a statue for more than five minutes after her husband left her, her hand still on her neck, the last place Stephen had kissed and the other hand clenched in anger at his parting word.

It was not that she was angry that he had abandoned her on their wedding night, she assured herself. It was only because the man had had the audacity to touch her so freely and she had allowed it, even sighing and gasping like a wanton woman.

But he's your husband, what would you have done? Her subconscious taunted her and she closed her eyes firmly, only to have the very same scene in the room play behind her lids but this time, he didn't just stop at her neckline. Penelope's breath and heart rate picked up at the thought as she thought about his hand delving below the fine silk, touching where no man had ever touched before, his surprisingly callused fingers gliding on her smooth skin, their slight pressure and unbelievable friction.

Her eyes shot open when a moan almost left her lips.

"What is wrong with me?" she murmured to herself, shaking her head to clear it and debating over whether she should call Rose and ask her to draw a bath like she had initially wanted or not.

They had just been discussing the very fact that she would be very grateful if Stephen didn't decide to exercise his husbandly rights on her that very night and it was ironical how she was angry that he hadn't just a few minutes later. Turning, she looked at herself in the full-mirror and tried to ascertain if her appearance had changed as much as she felt like she had changed inside but other than the silver gown, one that didn't help but remind her of Stephen's eyes, everything seemed the same.

Sighing, Penelope went to sleep a few minutes later not knowing why she felt a little disappointed and a lot of anger at her new husband.

The next morning, she was up before Rose came to her.

"There is a lot of talk downstairs," her maid and friend said, referring to the household servants.

"About what?" Penelope frowned, not understanding.

"That the Marquess was gone for most of the night and only came back when it was already dawn," Rose said meaningfully, and Penelope looked away.

"I don't know why everyone is talking about that. He is a free man, allowed to go and do whatever he may want," She shrugged, not wanting Rose to see that she still felt a little anger over his action last night. She hadn't wanted his company or him to stay with her last night, true but the man could've discreetly gone to his room instead of alerting the whole house about his departure, embarrassing her in front of the servants.

"They weren't very cruel. Everyone is really kind and happy here, as far as I could see and most of them were angry on your behalf. They know the circumstances of your marriage," Rose said, trying to mollify her as she took out her day dress, a green muslin gown that brought out her eyes but was a little revealing at the bodice.

"They know everything?" Penelope asked alarmed. She didn't know if she could even meet everyone's eyes if even they thought that she had been caught having a tryst with Fielding while a ball carried on just a few feet away from her.

"No!" Rose exclaimed, "Of course not," she said, getting her volume under control. "They just know that the match was forced upon the both of you by your brother."

Penelope breathed a sigh of relief. It was enough that her own family and her husband thought that way about her, she didn't want the servants to think that way about her too. Stephen was already halfway through his breakfast when she finally joined him.

"Husband," She spoke as she drew near, and he immediately stood to greet her, looking at her and then his eyes narrowing at her deep bodice just as his pupils flared.

"Wife," He nodded at her, his voice coming out a little deeper and grumblier than usual.

"I see you didn't wait for me," She smiled at him tightly as she sat, and he followed. A young boy rushed about and finally brought her breakfast in a hot plate.

"I didn't think you would be up early," He replied, brows raised as if surprised that she had called him out on it. She shouldn't have but she was just a little pissed, the anger at the events of the night still simmering on low.

"So, you do think sometimes?" She taunted and then immediately regretted it when his eyes shuttered. She was just about to open her mouth to apologize.

"What is this anger about? I had thought you would appreciate if I left you alone last night," He said thoughtfully, his voice just a little tight, betraying his own displeasure.

"Is this how this marriage is going to be?" Penelope shocked herself by asking and Stephen if his expression was any indication.

"I had thought..," He started to say and then shook his head, "I will be in your chamber tonight and every other night if that's not a problem?" He asked, left brow raised and a salacious smile on his lips. Penelope flushed and looked down at her plate.

"I want more than that," She said, looking up finally after a few minutes.

"More? What do you mean?" Stephen asked confused. Penelope herself had been confused about what the marriage meant to her until that very morning but just as she had descended the stairs and looked at her freshly shaved and bathed husband sitting at the table, she had known that she wanted to give the marriage a real chance, get to know Stephen and not watch her husband leave her back at the house while he spent his nights with a mistress.

"I want us to eat at least one meal together every day and spend some time with each other during the day too," She explained, looking anywhere but at him.

His fingers at her chin had her looking up at him as he smiled.

"You have yourself a deal Lady Penelope. You have my dinners and I will even more generous and give you an hour out of my day and in return I'll have your nights."

Penelope could feel as the blush climbed up her neck and covered her cheeks as Stephen kept a hold of her chin and his eyes held her captive otherwise, the

silver in them smoldering and shifting,
making her breath just a little faster.

He kept his promise that night and
for the next few weeks as well.

Chapter Ten

"What are you smiling about?" Bennet asked Stephen as he prepared his bath one morning.

"I'm not smiling. This is my normal face," Stephen replied, adjusting his expression immediately.

"Yes, and I'm the King of England," His valet rolled his eyes in response and Stephen sighed.

"I'm finally docking your pay this month," He warned him, picking up the sharp razor Bennet had laid out near the sink and starting to shave.

"And I have never really heard this before," The valet sounded almost bored. "Half of the house heard you and Lady Penelope in the library yesterday," Bennet said, wagging his brows and chuckling when Stephen shot him a deadly glare.

"Did you really think you're that quiet?" He asked as Stephen as he turned back to his sink. "You and the Marchioness have not left even a single piece of furniture in this house that you haven't christened, of course we are bound to notice."

Stephen ignored the man, not wanting to turn around and let the man see that he was all but flushed but it probably had more to do with him reliving all his memories from the library yesterday. No genius was needed to find out that the arrangement that they had made on their first breakfast was working out really very fine for him and his delectable marchioness.

The one-hour Stephen had allocated his wife had soon morphed into four almost every other day while the dinners were usually taken in their bed. It had been almost a month and Stephen were ready to admit that he had never felt such bliss before in his life and it was not just the passion that burned brighter between them every time.

It was also their conversations, occasional picnics and chess games and even the few society functions that they had attended over the past month. He could barely take his eyes off his wife at every one of them and she had blossomed into a happy, confident woman from a wallflower that she had once been.

While everything was great in all spheres, Stephen knew that they still never really talked about anything meaningful, he changed the topic every time they started to talk about their childhoods and Penelope had never brought up Fielding in front of him. Even though he was glad about that, the thought still pinched him every time and now the pinch had almost turned into a stab.

He didn't know how much longer he could hold it in and not question Penelope about what had really happened with the man and how was she over her love so soon.

"Have you told Lady Penelope about your father?" Bennet suddenly asked, as if picking the words from his very brain. "Everyone really loves her here and we don't want anything to make her upset."

"So, my past will be upsetting for her?" Stephen asked irritable. "Should I just change it?" He turned to look at his valet. "Oh wait, I can't."

"You're getting worked up about nothing. I just meant that you should tell her before she finds out about it from someone else and develops the wrong idea," Bennet shrugged, and Stephen wished that it was that easy. He had deliberately made sure that their talks remained superficial and not go any deeper than everyday things just because he could not imagine how he was going to tell his wife about his defining childhood. He knew there was a huge chance that she wouldn't understand.

He was a little subdued when Penelope joined him at dinner that night, not even standing up when she arrived at the table.

"Is everything alright?" She asked immediately, and Stephen cursed her perceptiveness.

"Why do you ask?" He questioned, looking at her with narrowed eyes.

"Just because you have been glaring at me since morning, haven't said a word to me all day and are eating your dinner as if it is the most delicious thing you have ever had," She replied flippantly. Stephen almost kissed her right there and then. He had really been avoiding her all day, but it hadn't been deliberate. Bennet's words and his own thoughts had been the main reason.

"I was not glaring at you, I was looking at how gorgeous you appeared in your blue gown all morning. I was just ogling," He corrected her, his mood improving as she laughed at that. He had realized at the very start of their marriage that his wife suffered with body image issues. While she was perfectly curvy and very beautiful, her mother and the society had ingrained it in her mind that she was fat, ugly-looking and needed to starve herself. The very belief had been cemented when she had made her debut in the society.

It had taken Stephen's constant teasing and compliments for almost a month to get her to eat normally and to not feel self-conscious whenever she wore a new dress.

"I would've come to dinner in that very gown, but I was helping the maids clean the attic and the gown was very dirty by the time we finished," She smiled, and Stephen smiled back. That was another thing he really adored about her even though it frustrated him to no end. He would often find him joining the help in their work. When he had asked her about it, she had told him that she felt strange just standing there while everyone else got busy at work. The servants didn't let her do much of anything, but she still was always helping them.

"Stephen," She said a few minutes later, just as he had relaxed for the first time since morning.

"Hmm?" He looked at her questioningly.

"When we were cleaning, we found a few old trunks. There was one really small, downtrodden trunk amongst them containing very strange things," She was saying, and Stephen felt as if the floor had been snatched from under his feet.

"Why did you touch those things?!" He snapped, unable to control his reaction.

"I was just..," Penelope started to say but he cut her off.

"Have I ever prodded and poked at your things?"

Penelope's face finally lost the smile and it was replaced by anger.

"I did not poke or prude at anything. I did not even know that the trunk belonged to you," She snapped as well, her green eyes spitting fire. "You rarely tell me anything about yourself and I have never even asked, why would I go searching through your things?!"-0

Chapter Eleven

Penelope was almost seeing red. It was true what she had said. She had never forced or needled Stephen about anything. Not his past or the fact that he never talked to her about anything personal. All of their conversations dealt with practical things and even though Penelope could feel the softness and the change in her husband when it came to her, she was also aware that their relationship was still very superficial.

"I'm not saying anything of the sort. You should just not meddle into things that are not your concern," He said, rubbing his hand over his nose but instead of pacifying her, his words ignited another fire in Penelope until she couldn't control the next words that slipped out of her.

"Oh, I would really like to know what concerns me according to you," She said tautly. "Do you, my husband, concern me or are you out of my sphere too?"

"Why are you making such a big deal out of all this?" Stephen asked, angry once again.

"I'm just trying to find out when you will accept me completely? When will I live in this house, not as a stranger, but as the mistress of the house and your wife?" Penelope demanded, tears starting to clog her throat.

"What more do you want me to do?" Stephen suddenly shouted. "I married you, brought you into this house and am trying to come to terms with so many things at once! How much more do you want me to suffer?!"

"I see," Penelope said quietly, the tears now flowing out of her eyes. "This marriage and me are both sufferings for you. My brother forced you into this marriage and now you're stuck. This marriage will never be more than that, will it?"

"Since you are such an expert on everything, why don't you figure this out for yourself too?" Stephen said, thundering away. His footsteps echoed in the hall long after he left as Penelope stood frozen on the spot for more than ten minutes, desolation and the feeling that nothing was ever going to get better, eating at her.

She was glad that she had given the servants the rest of the day off. She could just imagine the kind of talk their recent argument would've generated. Her motivation in giving them the day off was to get time to talk to Stephen, to serve him and to spend time getting to know each other in an intimate environment. All of that had fired off badly. She was still trying to think around everything that had happened when she heard the front door slam.

She ran all the way to the door, just to catch Stephen before he left for the night but by the time she got to the bottom of the stairs, he had already left. Penelope sat down at the very last stair herself and started to wonder where she had exactly gone wrong in life. The only answer she could think of was the season her brother had forced her to attend and then the marriage he had forced her to go along with.

Well, he should force me to be happy now too, she thought bitterly, wiping her tears and the thought hadn't completely gone out of her when someone knocked on the door. The sound was so foreign to Penelope that she was disoriented for a moment. The presence of servants had always been constant in her life and the butler had always been there to open doors and let people in that Penelope didn't know what she should do until the thought that maybe Stephen had come back prompted her to rush to the door.

She was so sure that it was her husband on the other side of the door that she opened the door up and already started to say,

"I have been waiting..," and stopped when she saw the one person she had thought and hoped fervently to not ever see again in her life.

"Hello Penelope," Lord Fielding smiled at her from the other side of the threshold.

"It's Lady Debrett," She corrected him and looked away, quickly trying to think of something to get rid of him. She had realized her mistake as soon as she had seen him.

Penelope knew that even Fielding would be wondering why she was opening the door herself and if he deduced that she was home alone, without servants or any help, she didn't want to think what would happen. The ballroom incident was still very fresh in her mind.

"Lady Penelope," He all but sneered but then suddenly, his face took on a very somber look. "I am sorry, but I don't come bearing good news."

Penelope's heart started beating at a staccato at his words. A thousand different scenarios ran through her mind but worry about her husband was first and foremost.

"What do you mean?" She demanded without any preamble.

"Stephen is badly injured. He got in a fight at the gaming hell and was fully into his cups when the fight broke out," He explained, and Penelope gasped.

"Where is he?!" She cried out, holding the jamb tightly until she feared her fingers were going to fall off.

"He is at a local infirmary, but his condition is not good. He is unconscious and while matters such as this do not concern women, his condition made me revaluate, especially since he has no one else to take care of him," He shrugged. Penelope's world was turning gray at the edges as she started offering prayers and almost demanding her husband's health from God.

"Will you take me to him?" She asked him, her voice shaken as she remembered that none of her servants were home and her brother's house was on the other side of town. Fielding was the last person she wanted to ask for help but since he had been caring enough to bring her the news, she was hopeful that he would get her there without any damage too.

"Of course, we can go right now," He said, grandly gesturing to his carriage standing in the driveway.

Penelope rushed into it without another thought, while her heart prayed,

'Please God let Stephen be okay. I haven't even told him how much I've come to care for him and love him. Please don't let anything happen to him when the last conversation we ever had was this one.'

Chapter Twelve

Stephen felt as if his head was being split open in the middle. He couldn't remember the last time he had drank as much but once glass of whiskey had led to another and then so on until he could barely remember why he had started drinking in the first place.

She had fallen asleep on one of the chairs in the gaming hell and didn't even know how much time had passed.

"We are closing my Lord. Everyone is gone, I thought you would want to call your carriage too?" A burly and large man stood in front of Stephen as he tried to speak up with his tongue that felt more like a sandpaper than an actual part of anatomy.

"What time is it?" He finally rasped out, his mind catching up with everything that had happened, ending up with his last memory of the card game he had been losing one after the other. The thought of Penelope's tears and the way he had left the house had an ache blossom in his chest. He had been so blinded with anger and embarrassed that she had found things he had never shown anyone, he had lashed out and hurt her in the worst way possible.

She had made life better for him, made him whole from the husk of the man he had once been and while he didn't know his exact feelings for her, he knew that he would absolutely prefer life with her than without.

Who am I fooling? I cannot even imagine life without her light and her innocence, he snorted as he got up unsteadily.

"Your carriage, my Lord?" The guard asked again, and Stephen grunted.

"I rode my stallion here."

"I'll get the stablemaster to bring it to the back and you can exit through the back door," He told Stephen, displeasure and disapproval apparent on his face and Stephen smiled. The expression reminded her of Penelope when she was angry at him over someone small such as holding her hand in front of the servants or not being the model of propriety she wanted them to be. His wife had a long way to go before she became comfortable with his rejection of the rules of the society.

The ride home was no less than agonizing as the movement of the horse made him feel as if someone was taking a hammer to his head. He had been told that it was past midnight and, in his estimation, he had been out of the house for more than seven hours. He had rehearsed his apology a few times on the way home and had also made another decision.

While their fight had been because of his own ego, he could also see that Penelope was right. He had accepted her as his wife, but he still did not trust her with his secrets, his fears and his past. He had been burned by the one person he should've been able to trust all his life when he had been an infant and he had never trusted another. Maybe it was time he opened up not just his house but also his heart and soul to Penelope. He also couldn't go another day without asking her what had really happened with Fielding. The event and the ones which had changed the course of their lives were nothing short of Godsend but there was still a large part of him that wanted to hear her negate everything, tell him that it had been a misunderstanding and maybe also that she could fall in love with him one day.

The desire to hear those words and feel that emotion from his wife surprised him but he realized that he had been angling for it ever since they had said their vows because he had fallen a little in love with the woman who had walked out of the church alone with her head held high that very day.

The next one hour was the most difficult one of his life. To not find Penelope in the house then be informed that she had left and that too with Fielding was his worst nightmare come true. He had wanted to call out the neighbor's butler, the man who had seen them last, for even uttering those words about his wife. He had him recount the event almost five times to make sure that Penelope wasn't being forced or if the man really was Fielding but everything the butler described was spot on.

His heart ached, and he wanted to lock himself in his study and not face the world for at least a week, but his mind rebelled it all. He justified that he would've seen the signs if she had been unhappy and even though images of his mother kept circulating in his mind, he ignored it all and got on his stallion once again.

"They went West?" He asked the man, his words coming out as lashes from the whip and even the man looked a little scared now. Stephen spurred on the horse as soon as he nodded. According to the butler, he had last seen them more than four hours ago but there really weren't a lot of places they could go in London. He decided to start with the most obvious ones. It was dawn when he admitted defeat.

Chapter Thirteen

Penelope tried as hard as could to dislodge the gag Fielding had stuffed in her mouth. For the past four hours, all she had done was chide herself for her stupidity and gullibility. She should've known that nothing Fielding said could be true.

If I ever get out of this hackney and make it home to Stephen, I'll never have another argument with Stephen, she promised herself but knew that it was probably all in vain. She had had no idea what Fielding had planned up until he told the hackney driver to take them as close to the Scottish border as he can. She had been as skeptical as the driver when he had announced them but now after four hours of struggling to get her hands free, she was almost resigned.

The hackney jerked once again, and this time Penelope tumbled to the other side of the dirty floor. Her hand collided with something and when she squinted her eyes to see what it was, new hope formed in her mind.

Fielding, the idiot, was sleeping on the lone seat and Penelope made sure that she remained deathly quiet as she worked on cutting the rope binding her hands with the small jagged and sharp metal edge at one side of the seat. The rope was a thin one and it took her almost half an hour to get her hands free and then came the rope binding her feet and the gag in her mouth. Once she was free, she deftly picked up the pistol from his pocket and then sharply rapped on the hackney and waited for the cab to stop. Fielding was so deep in sleep that he didn't even wake up.

****

It was twilight when Penelope had the hackney cab stopped in front of the townhouse. While there was a feeling of giddiness due to relief, she was also wary of what she was going to have to face inside. She hoped that no one had seen her leave with Fielding or there was going to a lot of damage.

"My Lady," the butler rushed towards her. "Are you alright?"

"I'm fine. Please see to it that this cab driver is paid full and well," she said, gesturing to the hackney driver and simply striding inside the door. If there was a price to pay for her actions, she wanted to just get it over it.

"Where is Lord Debrett?" she asked the maid who was standing just inside the door with her mouth agape, staring at her as if she had seen a ghost.

"H-his study, my Lady," the maid answered as if in a trance, and without waiting for her to recover or her own courage to desert her, Penelope rushed towards Stephen's study. She opened the door without knocking and utter chaos greeted her inside. The sturdy oak antique writing table had been overturned, all the drawers thrown every which way, the floor littered with broken furniture, paper, and anything else her husband had gotten his hands on. Numerous bottles of liquor were also part of the wild carnage and for a moment, Penelope stood frozen, horrified and scared once again.

"Did I not say that I was not to be disturbed?!" Stephen's shout broke her out of her trance as he picked up a heavy paperweight lying near his foot on the floor and hurled it at the bookcase on the opposite side of the room. Penelope flinched but then focused on him. He was sitting on the floor, facing away from her, his head in his hands and torn books and papers lying near his feet.

"Stephen?" Her voice almost came out a whisper as she finally managed to get the words out. His head whipped around, and the startling silver eyes focused on hers completely. There was no expression on his face. His eyes looked dead and his countenance made a shiver roll up her spine. He didn't say anything for the next thirty seconds, her heart counting the time with each hurried beat.

"Please let me explain," Penelope spoke up, breaking the utter silence as she moved into the room. If she expected him to say anything, she couldn't have been more wrong. His steady gaze remained steadfast on her, but he didn't utter a single word. Without waiting for any encouragement, Penelope hurriedly started her own tale.

"He told me you were at the infirmary and that he was going to take me there. I made a grave mistake in believing him," she started, and then told him every single detail up until the moment she had found the sharp extension in the seat of the hackney.

"I cut the bindings on my hand," She was now close enough for him to see the marks when she extended her arms towards him. "Once I got free, I picked up his pistol, bound his hands while he slept and once he was awake, I threatened the driver and then offered him double the wages Fielding had promised if he could bring me back here," she finished, and she may just have told the story to a marble statue because other than the occasional blinking, her husband hadn't even said one single word since she had arrived.

"Stephen?" Penelope gathered the courage and moved her hand over to his biceps, squeezing the taut fabric of his shirt there.

Her hand had barely touched the shirt when he suddenly pulled on her extended hand, jerking her straight and with finite force, smack dab into his body. The breath rushed out of her and then the tears started to fall. She had kept them at bay throughout the ride back, occupying her mind with the tension of whether Stephen was going to believe her or not.

"I'm so sorry," he whispered in her ear as he placed small, sweet kisses all over her face.

"What for?" Penelope asked, the tears and the sweetness of the combined with the relief making her heart feel lighter than it had in a long time.

"For the baseless argument we got into. You are my wife, my happiness and one of the few people I really respect," he said, moving back and looking into her eyes as he said that. "You do not have superficial importance in my life, you are my life."

His face and his eyes were so honest and earnest that Penelope couldn't control the tears that were continuously flowing from her eyes.

"I'm sorry too," she said, placing both her palms on either side of his face and looking into his eyes. "I should've waited for you to explain things to me when the time was right," she was saying but he shook his head to stop her right there.

"No, you were right. We were stuck in one place and we needed to move forward. I realized everything when I woke up drunk at the gaming hall but then I came home to an empty house. I've seen quite a lot in my life, but these were the worst few hours," Stephen told her, his eyes misty with unshed tears and voice rough with emotion.

"Will you tell me everything now?" Penelope asked. She was sick and tired of all the distance and the secrets between them. She wanted to disperse with them all now that life had given them a chance.

Stephen sighed and nodded.

"My mother kidnapped me when I was an infant. She was having an affair with vicar's son and had thought to use me for ransom from my father as she ran away," Stephen said, and Penelope couldn't stop the quick indrawn breath at the statement. Her own mother was not up for any motherhood awards but for any woman to do that to her own flesh and blood, she couldn't even imagine.

"As luck would have it, before she could ask for the ransom, her carriage upturned, and while her lover and her child escaped unscathed, she lost her life right upon impact. The lover, afraid and not knowing what to do, left me in an abandoned alley and ran for his life." He was saying the words with no emotion whatsoever, but Penelope could feel that the wounds were all still fresh. She didn't say a word, waiting for him to continue.

"My father found me eventually, but it was almost seven years later." He smiled at her widened eyes and open mouth and then shook his head ruefully. "I was safe, but I was the brightest student of the best street thief in London."

"How did-?" Penelope started to say but Stephen cut her off.

"He was the one who had found me in the alley and I would forever owe him my life for not just passing by and ignoring a baby's cry in an alley. He did not have enough money for even himself, but he took me in, raised me the only way he knew, and kept me alive until my father found me and

brought me home to his estate," Stephen
said, shrugging as he finished.

"Why did you not want to tell me all
this?" Penelope asked, emotions deepening
her voice. "This is the most incredible story
of resilience and bravery that I've heard,"
she said, amazed.

"You think so?" Stephen smiled as
he pulled her into his lap and gave her a
searing kiss on the lips.

"I know so. You have not let your
past hold you back and have rather learned
your lessons and made sure that life for you
is exactly how you want it to be. I don't
know if there is anything more wonderful
than that," she explained, and he smiled
once again. She wanted to box it up and
keep it somewhere close to her heart.

"I was given the title and the lands, I
think your womanly feelings are making me
out to be some sort of hero," Stephen

teased her, and Penelope playfully smacked him on the arm.

"Everyone knows that your father's estates were in a decline, he barely had enough money to run everything and he left it to you when bets were being placed on how soon you will go bankrupt," she reminded him. "You not only restored it all back to its glory in less than ten years but yours is one of the most profitable estates now."

"You know quite a lot about my handlings," Stephen said, flicking her nose. "I'm starting to think that you married me for my money." Penelope grinned and looked at him shyly.

"I married you because I had no other option, but I know why I want to stay married to you forever now," she said, and he raised his brow in his customary fashion.

"Because I love you," she whispered, her cheeks red and her eyes shining with sincerity. Stephen gave her the most blinding smile at her statement and took her face in his hands as he murmured the four words she felt like she had been waiting forever for,

"I love you too, wife."

They sat on the floor talking until it was almost noon the next day as Penelope told him everything about Fielding and Stephen vowed to make sure that the man never had the nerve to do the same things to another woman. Once all the talking was done, they fell asleep in the same position, hugging each other and none of the servants disturbed them as they cleaned the room around them.